BRICK CITY BLUES

SETH EDGARDE

BLACKBIRD BOOKS

NEW YORK • LOS ANGELES

A Blackbird Original, January 2017

Manufactured in the United States of America.

The events and characters depicted
in this book are fictional.

Cataloging-in-Publication Data

Edgarde, Seth.
Brick city blues / Seth Edgarde.
p. cm.
1. Newark (N.J.)—Fiction. 2. Newark International
Airport—Fiction. 3. Air travel—Fiction. I. Title.
PS3605.D4564 B75 2017 813'.6—dc23 2016960643

Blackbird Books
www.bbirdbooks.com
email us at editor@bbirdbooks.com

ISBN 978-1-61053-040-8

First Edition

10 9 8 7 6 5 4 3 2 1

BRICK CITY BLUES

Another trip to Albany, another three-hour layover in Newark. He didn't mind it at this point. An escape from the wife. *The wife*. It was a joke. The divorce papers had come through a year ago. All they needed to do was sign and file them with the county clerk. But they never did. He had opened the envelope while she sat sipping her coffee in the kitchen. "The papers," he said, holding them up. "Oh," she said. Then they looked at each other, and he shoved them in the desk drawer. They're still there, and the two of them are still legally married, still living together in the same posh Miami condo. They even had sex once in a while.

It had never been her idea to get divorced. It was all him, so she was happy enough to keep the status quo. He had thought it was about keeping up appearances. She was like that. It was one of the things about her that drove him nuts. But now he wasn't so sure. He caught her sobbing in the bathroom the night before last, and she tried to cover it up when he walked in to see if she was alright. It made him wonder. He was glad to be out of there. Every Monday up; every Thursday back. With three hours in Newark in between. A mini vacation, right there in the Brick City, where he was born on a cold fall day forty-seven years ago. He'd go have a drink at the bar.

He watched the woman in front of him wheeling her carry-on, lavender. Nice round ass, he thought. A little big, but nice. As he moved past her, he glanced out the corner of his eye. Nice enough face, a little plain maybe, but she looked smart. No makeup, small, oval, wire-rimmed glasses. She was pale with high cheekbones that gave her a slightly severe demeanor, but that was offset nicely by her rolling, lush brown locks, parted in the middle. He guessed she was in her early forties. A schoolteacher maybe. She had that librarian look. Nice chest too, he thought, as she disappeared from view. He grinned. *There goes another one I'll never have.*

When he hit the bar, he slipped his briefcase down in front of the stool, pinning it with his foot against the wood veneer at the front of the bar. *Constant contact.* He didn't even want to think about what would happen if he lost it.

He caught the bartender's eye. He recognized him by now, even though this was only his third trip up. The man was grey and thin, with black plastic-framed glasses down on his nose. He looked up over the top of the magnifying lenses as he wiped a glass, lifting his head slightly and holding up his index finger to signal that he'd be there in a minute. He could tell that the man recognized him too.

"Scotch and soda, right?" The bartender finally smiled.

"You got it."

He watched him pour the shot of Red, and he thought about his wife. She hated that he liked such a lowbrow drink. She preferred overpriced wine from Napa or, even better, France. He was sure she couldn't tell the difference. He handed over his credit card and took his first sip, noticing the woman with the purple carry-on and the nice ass sitting alone at a table across from the bar.

He continued to sip as he watched her. She looked at the menu on the table, crossed her legs, and pulled out her phone, reading or checking her email. The waiter came over, and she ordered something, pasting on a polite smile in the process. She pulled out a book—he couldn't make out the title, but it was thick and had the unadorned cover of a serious work of non-fiction—and she began to read. A moment later, the waiter brought her drink. It looked like plain old lemonade. Another fake smile, and she began to drink through the straw as she read.

Without warning, she looked up and caught him staring at her. It was just an instant, before he turned back to the bartender, nonchalant as could be, and ordered another S&S, but he knew he was busted. He could also see from the way her mouth moved, parting just a little at the lips, that she recognized him from before, when he walked past her in the terminal corridor.

When he turned back from the bartender again, he looked straight at her, unable to suppress a smile, but her nose was already back in her book. If they'd have made eye contact, he would have gone over and talked to her, but the moment was gone, and now the briefcase popped back into his head and a flash of panic as he moved his foot, unable to find it until he realized only a split second later, that he'd never lost contact. His second drink landed on the bar in front of him, and he swallowed it in two gulps, sliding his thin, 6'4" frame off the stool and grabbing the briefcase as he signaled for his tab. He left cash and a ten-dollar tip, swinging around and catching a last glimpse of the woman at the table before heading off, back out into the terminal.

He walked around a bit, watching the people— flight attendants in tight skirts and heels, walking in bunches with tall, good-looking pilots; janitors and cleaning women in grey uniforms keeping the place tip-top; business people with laptops and cell phones, in suits, like him. But most probably *not* like him; families with children. Definitely not like him. His hand sweated around the handle of his case.

He made his way past another bar and towards the food court. The place was a wonder. Who'd have thought—the United terminal at Newark Airport. Bookshops, bars, and restaurants. A great place to cool your jets, so to speak, hang out, relax, read a book. Flirt with a stranger even. Here in this little cocoon, past TSA security, apart from the world, a gussied-up limbo, complete with a limitless supply of Johnnie Walker Red, friendly bartenders, and nice-looking women to watch.

There was tomorrow, and his appointment in Utica. But that was tomorrow. For now, he'd go have a burger and relax. He wasn't much of a reader, but maybe he'd even go get a book.

He walked up to Custom Burger and ordered off the iPad. He thought about getting Italian or maybe even a shish-kabob but couldn't resist the overstuffed burger with the jalapeños and the pepper jack cheese. His wife was a good cook, but he longed for that burger and coke, the perfect cap to his double shot of JW Red. He got the burger, sat down, and sank his teeth in. He felt great. Free as a bird with just the right buzz. He finished chewing, took a gulp of Pepsi, and looked up. And there she was, *again.* Hardly surprising, he realized. Even in this wonderland, there were only so many places to go to kill your layover. And there was a logic to it: Get off your plane, have a cocktail, maybe read a little, and grab a bite.

She was eating a salad. He looked right at her, but even when she looked up, she didn't acknowledge him. She seemed to look right past him. Maybe she didn't see him. Her glasses were thick, and she seemed cold and distant. And he suddenly wanted to know, to know if it was just a façade, or if there was someone deeper there. Her eyes flicked to him for a second, and he knew she saw him, even as she turned her attention back down to her salad.

He finished his burger and the last of his drink, threw away the garbage, and headed back down the corridor. He checked out the shops, considering whether he needed a new case for his phone before deciding against it. Then he hit the men's room, taking a stall to relieve himself instead of a urinal so he could lock the door and keep an eye on the briefcase while it was out of his hands.

Back out in the terminal, he spied Brookstone and looked at the gadgets through the window—he was a sucker for those middle-class conveniences they sold there—but he decided not to go in. He hated when the salespeople would ask if they could help, and he didn't really feel like dealing with a purchase like that.

So he walked down a bit further and headed into the bookstore. He was an indifferent reader, generally sticking to non-fiction when he did bother, preferably sports stories or maybe true crime now and then. He preferred real life. He had that in common with his wife. But here he was, plucking over the titles at Hudson Booksellers, leafing through Malcolm Gladwell's latest. It looked interesting, a tome on underdogs overcoming superior odds to prevail in the end, but he knew he wasn't going to buy it. He'd never read it. Not even there in the airport. He was still looking at it as he closed it and slipped it on the shelf, walking away in the process, head turning forward, when he ran right into a woman walking in the opposite direction. His hand touched her breast as he brought it down from the shelf and then they bumped right into each other. He grabbed her to stop her from falling backwards, and he saw. *Her. Again.*

Then, without missing a beat, "Well I just keep running into you, don't I?"

She smiled, and her face lit up. Her features looked even more chiseled. She wasn't really pretty, but she looked kind and intelligent, and certainly not bad looking. And he could see that she was startled but amused and recovering fast.

"We have to stop meeting like this," he said.

It was sort of a dumb line, but they both laughed, and his brain finally processed the feeling of her breast on his hand—he'd gotten a pretty good feel, and they both knew it—and he was still holding her shoulders, now finally letting go.

They stood for a second, face-to-face. He was always the gentleman—he'd never do anything like that on purpose—but it was too late to ask if she was ok. And that was exactly what made it ok.

"Listen, you want to go get a drink?"

She hesitated for a second. He could tell she didn't get asked out very often and was unsure, defenses still up.

"I know a great bar around the corner," he said, teasing her just enough, playful but persistent.

He was about to let it go, throw out a dumb line about how it was nice bumping into her, and be on his way, then she pursed her lips with a little smile and raised her eyebrows just a little, and he knew he was almost there.

But then she gave him that look, sweet and sad. "I'd love to, but maybe some other time," she told him. "I have a flight to catch."

Letting him down easy, was that it? It was ridiculous. *Some other time.* Like when? Tomorrow? Next week? Next year? He was annoyed and felt like asking her. He wouldn't, of course, but he decided to press her just a little more, make her squirm, give in or come clean. "When's your flight?"

It caught her off guard, and she looked at him blank for a second. "Uh, five o'clock."

"Well it's not even two," he said, even though it was a few minutes after. "You won't need to be at the gate until at least 4:30. That's more than two and a half hours."

Then, like a drowning woman, struggling to save herself but getting in deeper, she confessed. "Well, actually, they start boarding at five o'clock. The flight's not till 5:35."

She smiled at him, but it was the wistful grin of someone who'd been outmaneuvered, trapped herself, wasn't used to it, and didn't like it.

Then he smiled back at her, wide and warm. His wife always said those big white teeth and baby blues made her melt, and he could see it was having its effect.

"Come on, let's go sit for while, have a drink." Then he looked right into those impenetrable brown eyes and opened his just a little wider. "Unless you want to keep wandering around here running into each other for the next three hours."

He could see she hadn't thought of that. *Yeah, that would be awkward.* She nodded. "Ok, one drink."

One drink. That annoyed him too. He knew she didn't have anywhere to go. Why not sit and relax? It wasn't like he could ask her back to his place. You couldn't do much more than hold hands without getting arrested in an airport terminal these days. Secured area and all. It made him think about the contents of that briefcase, and he smirked.

"What are you smiling about?" she asked, smiling at him herself as they walked down to the bar.

He realized she thought he was smiling at having persuaded her to go to the bar with him, and that made him smile even more. She noticed, and the way her face lit up made his annoyance dissipate. When they got to the bar, he thought to take a table, but his instincts told him to stick with the bar. It seemed less threatening, and she was already skittish.

"What would you like?" he asked, sliding back onto the barstool as he slipped his case down and pinned it with his foot.

"A lemonade would be great," she said.

Oh brother, he thought. But the truth was he didn't mind skipping a third shot just then. Still, he had to suppress a smile. He looked over and caught the bartender's eye. Like a good bartender, he saw that he was back, this time with a girl, and pretended like he didn't know him, like he hadn't already had a couple, picked up a girl, and came back for more.

He'd probably seen it all, that bartender, there in the middle of Terminal C, with the married men and women on their business trips, the singles on their getaways, people shuttling to and from funerals and family trips, cheaters and crooks, people on the trip of a lifetime and routine commuters, and those carrying the weight of the world on their shoulders and trying not to show it. And every other piece of humanity in between.

"Lemonade and a Coke," he told the man.

"Pepsi ok?"

"Sure."

She slid onto the stool next to him, and the bartender laid their drinks down on the bar. He handed over his credit card and shot the bartender a glance. The bartender winked at him and smiled just a tad, as the woman was busy with her first sip, too preoccupied to notice. *Good luck, buddy,* he seemed to say. *And don't worry, I'll keep the tab open.*

He noticed his name tag for the first time. Ralph.

"Thanks, Ralph," he said, lifting his glass of Pepsi, and the man smiled full on before turning away.

He looked over at her on the barstool next to him and held up his glass to clink, but she was in mid-sip. She stopped, swallowed what was in her mouth, and touched her glass to his with a sheepish look in her eye for having forgotten about the silly ritual.

She looked at him, somewhere between thoughtful and stern. "You know him?"

It took him a second to realize what she meant. Because he called him by name. "It's on his name tag."

Her expression changed as she nodded in realization. He liked her face. It was very expressive. He noticed her thick glasses, delicate gold-rimmed ovals, a kind of no-frills accessory that still showed a touch of style. She was so the opposite of his wife, Pam, who was petite and always meticulously put together. Suddenly he realized she was looking right at him.

"You know, I don't even know your name!"

"Nicholas," he told her.

She put down her lemonade and stuck out her hand. He shook it. It was cold and wet from the sweat on the glass, but he liked touching her. "Vicky," she told him. "It's Victoria, actually." She licked lemonade off her lips. "But I like Vicky." She shot him a glance as she took another sip. "I look enough like a nineteenth century schoolmarm already."

Definitely a teacher. "What do you do, Vicky?"

"I work on a road crew," she said, dead serious.

"Really?"

She grinned from ear-to-ear. A little revenge for cornering her into a drink in the first place. "No." She lifted her eyebrows. "No, I don't work on a road crew." She chuckled then took another sip, a little too pleased with herself. "I teach. French literature. Up at

Cornell. That's where I'm coming from, Ithaca, New York."

Yeah, of course, even better. A professor. The bookish look and slightly geeky demeanor. The crisp way that she spoke, erudite and precise, with perfect elocution.

"How about you?"

He looked at her, Pepsi still untouched, ice slowly melting. "I'm a contractor," he said.

She nodded, and he wasn't quite sure she knew what that meant. Too blue-collar, probably, and he suddenly felt a need to impress her.

"I'm working on a project for the Department of City Planning up in Albany. They're renovating a bunch of houses in the historic district, and they needed a contractor who knows about conservation." He knew he was laying it on a bit thick, but he could tell she was impressed. He grinned at her, flashing those pearly whites and blue eyes. "I also came in with the lowest bid."

She smiled. "I thought about being an architect. When I was in college, I was obsessed with Second Empire design. But I can't do math, and then I fell in love with Zola, and here I am!"

Who the fuck is Zola? He was about to ask if that was her boyfriend, when she continued.

"It's hard to appreciate his writing in translation. It's just not the same." She took a sip then looked over at him. "Don't get me wrong, I like Balzac— I wrote my thesis on Balzac!—but there was something so human about Zola. I wish I'd met him."

He wasn't sure what to say. He didn't have the heart to tell her that he'd never heard of either one of them, but she just kept on talking. He decided then and there that he wanted to kiss her.

"Have you ever read any Balzac?"

He couldn't stand it any longer. "I studied civil engineering in school. B.S. and M.S. Right down the road at NJIT."

She smiled at him wryly as if to say, *oh, one of those!* "I'll lend you *The Human Comedy* sometime. I think you'd really like it."

Yeah, sometime. It made him think, think about what it would be like to read it in front of a fireplace with her by his side, staring through those thick glasses at page after page of whatever book she was reading when she was sitting there alone before. It was a pleasant image, and he held it for a moment longer, savoring the brief silence. He decided he liked Vicky whatever her last name was. And he was glad to be having a drink with her there at the bar in Terminal C. Even if he'd probably never see her again.

"Have you ever been married?" She could see that his finger was empty.

He looked over at her. "Long story."

So he told her. Everything. Even the part about how he caught his wife crying a couple of nights ago. Maybe it was because she was a woman, a stranger who he'd never see again. Maybe he just needed to get it off his chest. At any rate, he didn't want to talk about his "work" anymore, and he sure as hell didn't want to talk about another French writer he'd never heard of.

She was a good listener, empathetic and kind. "She's still in love with you," she told him, and it made the blood run out of his face. "Do you still love her?"

He looked at her, eyes wide, then, when it was too much, he looked back down at the ice meltings at the bottom of his empty glass. "No. I mean, I care about what happens to her, but no. No, I don't love her anymore."

He thought about her for a moment. She was fifty-two, five years older than he, but she was still beautiful, petite, with a great body, dark features, and creamy white skin. It confused him for a moment, and he tried not to show it.

Finally, he looked up at Vicky. "How about you?"

"No, never married. Not even close." She smiled. "I guess I'm not the type."

He wasn't sure if that was a bitter remark or a projection of freedom.

"Well you're certainly pretty enough." He couldn't believe he'd said it even as the words were coming out of his mouth.

She blushed and seemed to have her breath taken away for a second. Then she looked at him and said "Thank you," before looking back down at her own empty glass. It was a sweet moment, allowed to be innocent by the circumstances—a brief interaction between strangers in an airport bar—and they both seemed to appreciate it.

She told him more about herself, that she was headed down to D.C. to work on a long-overdue project, an etymological dictionary of Provençal, the first of its kind in the English language. Her parents were in their seventies and lived just outside of DC, not too far away, over in Maryland, where she grew up.

She was interesting, and fun to talk to, and, he decided, had the kindest face he'd ever seen. He told her he'd lettered in basketball and baseball at NJIT and had even been drafted by the Detroit Tigers, which was actually true.

"I'm impressed," she told him.

"Don't be," he told her back. "They didn't pick me up 'till the sixteenth round. I'd never have made it to the majors."

She smiled at his modesty, and he smiled back at the kind eyes behind the wire-rimmed glasses.

Then, all of a sudden, it was time to go. She slid off the bar stool and, in a moment more true than impulsive, kissed him on the cheek.

Then she flashed a sad expression with her eyebrows. "I've got to go," she said. Then, breaking a smile, "It was wonderful meeting you."

"You too."

Then she turned and left, and the moment was gone.

He thought about her all the way to Albany. Her big brown eyes and her round ass. He should've gotten her number. But it was ridiculous. She was a stranger in an airport. He'd never see her again. He needed to put her out of his mind. He had a meeting and a drop tomorrow.

The briefcase was tucked under the seat in front of him. He needed to take a leak, but it would be too weird for him to take it with him, and there was no way he was leaving it unattended. Even though it was only for a few minutes. Even though it was locked.

When he landed, he picked up his rental car, a mid-sized Ford, and headed to the motel on the way out of town.

It was gold and smelled new, and he suddenly thought of Pam, his wife. He reached for his phone when it rang there in his hand. Pam.

"Hi there," he said, holding the phone to his ear with one hand and driving with the other.

"Hi," she replied. "How was your trip?"

"Good. I just landed. I'm in the car now."

There was a pause, and he knew what was coming next.

"I miss you."

Jesus Christ. He had the urge to say "me too," but he didn't, because he didn't miss her. Not really. And he didn't want her to get the wrong idea. He'd probably touch her face if he were there, and they'd end up in bed, but he was 1,500 miles away, and she was just another distraction that he didn't need.

"Listen, I've got to go. I'm pulling up to the motel. I'll call you later, okay?" He wasn't, and he wouldn't.

"I said I miss you."

"Me too." He could have kicked himself for saying it, but he just didn't have the energy for a long discussion right then. So it was the path of least resistance. It would have been better if she'd actually said "I love you." Then he could have just said it back and had it be the truth, even if it wasn't exactly the kind of love she wanted. Even if it was no longer the kind of love any real woman would actually want from a man.

Then they said goodbye, and he was alone again with his thoughts. Damned if Vicky from Terminal C wasn't right. He should have known. She's a woman and a stranger looking in from the outside, and she saw: *She's still in love with you.* He could hear her saying it. And suddenly, he didn't know. But he couldn't think about it. So he turned on the radio and made his way down the airport access road to the Motel 6.

He'd spend the night there and head out early for the drop in Utica. Then back to Albany for his meetings. He'd check into the Renaissance downtown tomorrow night.

In some ways, he preferred the Motel 6. No pretentious idiots fawning over him. Just an anonymous check-in, clean towels, and a wake-up call the next morning that he didn't really need.

There were a couple of fast food places on the way, but he wasn't hungry. He just wanted to find his room, maybe catch a little of the game on ESPN, and sack out.

When he finally did make his way to the check-in, it was the fat girl behind the desk. If she lost about fifty pounds, she'd be pretty, he thought to himself, but he was glad to see her anyway. She always gave him a quiet room and a nice smile. The older man who was sometimes there was much less friendly, and he smelled.

When he got to his room, he finally got to take that piss, but he ended up skipping the game and going straight to bed. He was surprised to be thinking of his wife as he fell asleep, but it wasn't pleasant, and he had bad dreams, though he couldn't remember them when he woke up.

The first thing he did when his eyes opened was reach underneath the bed for the briefcase. Still there.

By the time the wake-up call came, he was already showered and dressed. After a drive-thru Egg McMuffin and some coffee, he was on his way. An hour and a half later, he was parked outside of Jimmy's Café on

Genesee Street in Downtown Utica. He wanted to pop the briefcase open and double check it, but he didn't dare, not out there in the open. So he grabbed it off the front seat and went inside. Last booth on the right, adjacent to the counter, same as usual. Jimmy was there waiting. Three or four other thugs were scattered about the place and a few customers too. It was hard to tell the difference.

Jo Jo was by the door, as usual, and he handed him the briefcase to take in the back. Then he headed to Jimmy and the booth at the end.

He stuck out his hand and they shook as he sat, sliding across the red vinyl seat.

"How you doing, Nick?"

He never went by Nick, even when he played ball. It was always Nicholas. But he never corrected him.

"Doing good," he said.

The waitress came over, and Nicholas looked over at her. He hadn't seen her before. She was older, tall and skinny, with a body that would suit him well, though her face was a bit ragged. He saw her name tag: Linda.

"Coffee, black," he told her.

She looked over at Jimmy, who waved her off.

"Thanks, Linda," Nicholas said, flashing those pearly whites, and she smiled back, rolling her eyes and even shaking her head.

Both men watched her walk.

"That one's off limits," Jimmy told him.

And he knew he'd been there, even though he was married, and she really was off limits.

He brought his hands up on the Formica table top. It was sticky and matched the smell of the place: short-order fry grease and fake syrup with a vague hint of tomato sauce and garlic. The Utica mob. A cheap knockoff of the goombas from Brooklyn and the Bronx. And they knew it. Right down to the greasy café standing in for the red velvet Italian restaurants and the well-worn waitress doubling for the olive-skinned beauty with the sexy doe eyes.

"Enough talk about where we'd like to stick our dicks."

He liked Jimmy even less than the rest of Utica mob. He got back to the briefcase. "I didn't have a chance to count it."

"It's ok. I trust you," Jimmy said, looking him in the eye, even though he trusted nobody. "When do you meet with Gorman?"

"Thursday, before I fly back. The inspection's this afternoon. It'll give me tomorrow to write the report."

Jo Jo stuck his head out from the back and gave the okay sign.

Jimmy saw and nodded then looked back at Nicholas. "Good. If you need anything, let me know."

He nodded back and started to get up, when Linda came over with the coffee.

"I'll take it to go, please."

Picking up the empty briefcase on the way out, sipping his black coffee, Nicholas looked over the place and the assortment of mob goons, wise guys, and over-ripe customers. Definitely Jonesing with the downstate boys, number two but trying harder. And that's what made them dangerous. He knew he wasn't short on the drop, but he was still nervous every time he came in here, surrounded by men who had something to prove. When he started his car and pulled away, he let out a sigh of relief.

He continued to sip his coffee as he drove through downtown Utica. It was a 19th century time capsule, quaint, with red brick buildings, mom and pop shops, and a nice helping of Victorian architecture. It was a far cry from Miami, as were the rolling green hills on the way back to Albany, speckled with the turning autumn leaves. It was a far cry from Newark, too, where he was born and grew up. But here he was, dropping 50 G's every week to a second-rate thug like Jimmy in a greasy café in Utica. He'd get his own envelope later, from Badillos, back in Miami.

In the meantime, he had to get back to Albany, to the row houses that he was helping to restore in the Historic District. The inspector was due today, and he had to make sure everything was going smoothly. Of course, the inspector was on Jimmy's payroll, so it was all rubber stamped without so much as a second glance. But it needed to at least look good. The state building commissioner would be asking about it when they had breakfast Thursday morning, there at the Radisson, and Nicholas would give him the report before he flew back to Miami. He'd be back the next Monday, with another 50 large, and there'd be another rubber stamp, another breakfast meeting, and another fake report. And back in Miami, another envelope from Badillos.

It was a sweet deal. The city had solicited the state historic commission to apply for a federal grant to restore Albany's Historic District. When the money came through, it was even more than they had hoped for. Jimmy greased his wheels and reached out to the Cuban mafia in Miami. They'd supply cheap Chinese-made knockoffs of all the raw materials and finishings, bringing it in through South America and charging full price, pocketing the difference and splitting it with the boys in Utica, with plenty left over to pay off all the cogs.

They just needed a point man, a contractor who knew about conservation and restoration and was willing to play ball. Colón had set it all up. Nicholas had been an engineer and then a contractor in New Jersey and Miami and even ran an antique distributorship at one point. He had done several historic restorations in New Jersey and, later, in Miami and was a bit of an expert on Victorian architecture. Colón brought him to Badillos. It was a second career for him, but the boys in Miami didn't ask too many questions. They knew he was getting divorced and that he was tight on cash. They trusted Colón, and that was enough. The fact that he had a pretty wife who knew about antiques and design didn't hurt. The boys in Miami were a tough bunch but predictable. But Jimmy, he was a loose cannon.

He thought about it all on the way into town. He was always impressed driving into Albany. It was pretty and much more of a real city than anyone downstate would ever think, if they ever thought about it at all. And it had history. It also had more than its fair share of crooked pols. He drove by the Empire State Plaza, past the state capitol with its Romanesque design, and past the Radisson, where he'd check in later, and on to Pearl Street, then down towards the riverfront to the third house down, the old Victorian row house with the red door.

He parked the car in front and was surprised to see the door open. When he walked in, Jasper, the building inspector, was already looking around.

"Looks pretty good," he said, looking up at the molding on the ceiling, glancing sideways at Nicholas.

Nicholas looked up, expecting the worst, but it wasn't. It did look pretty good. He didn't answer, grabbing a chair instead and standing on it to get a closer look. It looked good up close too. He got down, and looked around further, barely noticing the man there with him.

He checked the paneling—good solid cherry, probably from another house, but refinished to perfection. And the new banister that had gone in since last week. Also top quality and impeccable workmanship. He could see the rolls of wallpaper lined up in the corner. The same. Beautiful, flawless, and expensive.

Finally, he looked over at Jasper. He'd met him before, seeing him briefly at a few different locations as the houses were being stripped down. He didn't pay him much attention. Just another jerk on Jimmy's payroll.

"It looks perfect," he said, trying to gauge his reaction.

"Yeah, it looks great," he said, matter-of-fact, checking a couple of boxes on his clipboard, before tearing the top copy off and handing it to Nicholas. "I can't wait to see it when it's all done."

Nicholas took the report—he'd give it to Gorman later on—and looked at it, still puzzled but trying not to show it. All the right boxes were checked, indicating everything was up to spec, up to code, and on schedule, with only a small note at the bottom: "Door inserts on order."

He looked over at the adjacent double-doors leading in to the living room. Plywood panels were sitting where the ornate carved inserts would eventually go.

He couldn't figure it. They were supposed to be cutting corners, but it looked like a restoration for the Queen of England. And Jasper didn't seem to have a clue. He couldn't think about it right then. He'd just play dumb. This wasn't his game. He delivered the money and got the inspection. He'd have his meeting with Gorman, pass along his own report, and get his envelope in Miami, then do it all over again the next week. He'd tell Colón, that was for sure. Let him handle it. Maybe that's all Jasper was doing. He had to notice. Or did he?

"Thanks, Bill," he said, pasting on a smile and looking the man in the face for the first time. He was a tall man, though not as tall as he was, with a gray moustache and horned-rimmed glasses.

"No problem. Take it easy. See you next week." And he was out the door.

Nicholas decided to take a look around. He opened the double doors to the living room, checking the fit and finish then stepping across the threshold, feeling the floor through his thin-soled Italian leather shoes. He scanned the room, taking in the molding as he went for the fireplace, which had just been refinished.

Upstairs was a bit rougher. There was only one bathroom, and the fixtures weren't in yet, but he could see the new sink lined up against the wall and the toilet there next to it. Refinished originals with all new internals, just like he'd ordered. And the bedrooms, though on the small side for modern tastes, were already painted in a dazzling array of colors in the Victorian style. It was like candy to the eye.

He went back down and headed out, turning back and taking in the place at a glance. It was less than half done, but he could imagine how it would look: Tight, clean, and colorful, with old-school care and craftsmanship that would exude elegance, quality, and taste. In a word, class. Not to mention money. He'd seen multi-million dollar renovations in Manhattan that didn't look as good as this townhouse was shaping up to be. He'd trade his Miami condo for it in a minute.

It was late afternoon, and he decided to leave his car and take a walk down to the riverfront. It was pretty, with the State Plaza off to his left with the sun setting behind it, throwing its spectrum of dying light onto the Hudson before him. Walking along the water, he still couldn't figure it. But it didn't matter. He'd grab dinner at his favorite pub over on Pearl street, go back to the Radisson, and write his report. He'd say how great everything looked, just like he was supposed to, only it would actually be true. He'd give the report to Gorman over breakfast the following morning then head out to the airport and back to Miami.

Gorman would only be half-listening, sucking down his coffee and eggs, feeding his fat belly, waiting for his own envelope from Jimmy, or the boys in Miami, or whoever else was supposed to be greasing this particularly greasy cog. Or maybe he'd gotten that wrong too. And suddenly, he just didn't care.

By the time his plane took off, he'd stopped thinking about it. He was looking forward to landing in Newark and heading over to his favorite bar in Terminal C for a shot of Johnnie Walker Red. You couldn't get a drink on the little puddle-jumpers, like the one he was on, that shuttled all over the northeast, but there was always Terminal C. Good old Newark. He had another three-hour layover. And he didn't have to worry about that damned briefcase on the way back—it was empty.

Stepping off the plane, he headed straight for the bar. On the way, his eyes caught the woman in front of him. Nice. He started to move past her when he noticed the glint of gold-rimmed eyeglasses. Then the purple suitcase she was pulling behind her.

"Vicky," he said, slowing up next to her.

She turned almost directly into him, the two of them still walking, now side-by-side. Her face opened with surprise. She recognized him right away but stumbled for a moment before spitting out his name. "Nicholas!"

He smiled at her, sly and friendly, like he knew her much better than he really did. "Just heading to the bar for a drink."

She smiled back at him, and it made him even more glad to see her. "Is that an invitation?"

"Only if you let me buy."

She pursed her lips with a mix of bemused gratitude and affection, like it was a more generous offer than it really was. She was certainly making up for the reticence she had last time. "I'll meet you there in five minutes."

He got it. She needed to use the bathroom. So did he. It was a huge relief not to have to worry about that briefcase. He thought about it when he was standing at the urinal. Then he put it out of his mind.

As he made his way to the bar, he took in the people for the umpteenth time. There was a janitor he recognized but who didn't seem to recognize him. Or at least paid him no attention. Stewardesses and pilots, passengers and airline workers. And somewhere in the crowd, a woman named Vicky.

As he approached the bar, he thought to take a table. He was sure he could do that now without scaring her off, but he took a stool at the bar anyway. He saw Ralph, with his back to him, serving a customer at the other end of the bar. It was an odd thing, but he felt a sort of loyalty towards the man. Like they were in it together, there in Terminal C, and he didn't want to stiff him on his tip, giving it to some waiter instead.

Vicky came a moment later and she slid up on her barstool, unaware of his internal debate, just as Ralph came over and Nicholas gave him a smile.

"Hey, Ralph."

"Pepsi, right?" and then he looked at Vicky without missing a beat. "And a lemonade."

"Hey, you're good!"

He smiled at Vicky, but Nicholas interrupted. "Actually, I'll have a double shot of Red."

Vicky jumped in. "Well, then maybe I'll have a white wine." Then she looked at Ralph and added, "Can you bring it over to us?" pointing at the tables.

"Sure thing."

Nicholas waited until her back was turned and slipped Ralph a ten. Ralph took it and gave him a wink.

A minute later, a waiter followed them over and placed their drinks on the table in front of them as they took their seats. Nicholas handed him his credit card. "Keep it open." Then he turned his attention to Vicky, who was already looking at him. They locked eyes, and she gave him a warm smile.

"Well this is a pleasant surprise!"

She took a sip and so did he, not bothering with a toast this time.

"Yeah, I wasn't expecting to see you again," he said, not meaning to express it exactly like that, but she didn't seem to mind.

"I always think I'm going to get work done, but I just end up walking around the terminal," she said, as if it were a guilty confession.

"You come here often?" he asked, grinning at his own cheekiness.

She raised her eyebrows, slightly amused, but only slightly. "Twice a week, actually. Ithaca to Washington every Monday, and back to Ithaca on Thursday." She took another sip. "Connecting through Newark. Three hour layover each way."

Now he raised his eyebrows. "Me too. Twice a week. Miami to Albany every Monday and back to Miami on Thursday. Three hour layover each way."

"No way!" she seemed genuinely excited, like it was the work of the gods or the invisible hand of fate or kismet in action. "What time are your flights?"

They compared flights and realized that they landed and took off within minutes of each other on both days.

Then they worked their way through a second round of drinks and talked for the next two hours before grabbing a bite at the food court and parting ways. He told her about the houses up in Albany, and she told him about the class she was teaching in French Lit and the project she was working on in DC, a twenty-two volume etymological dictionary of Provençal, funded jointly by the French government and the Lycée Français. She was assistant project head, and he was very impressed, but she didn't seem happy about it. So he asked, and she told him she'd tell him about it next time, and that excited him. Then it was time to go.

"Can I have your number?" he asked, and she hesitated.

"Well, I'll see you here on Monday," she told him. Then she looked at her watch—she still wore one—small and gold and feminine. "I've got to go. And so do you." And she began to move away from him, still standing there at the food court, until he had to shout to make himself heard.

"I don't even know your last name!"

"Scardo!"

"Will you have dinner with me on Monday, Vicky Scardo?!" he asked almost yelling through the people.

"Yes!" she said. "It's a date!"

And then she disappeared down the hall and into the crowd, purple suitcase in tow.

By the time she landed in Ithaca, she was kicking herself for not having given him her number. She didn't get asked out that often, and she really liked him. But what was the point? They lived in separate cities and had separate lives. And he was still married for god's sake! At any rate, she had a date with him on Monday. It scared her a little, but what could happen in an airport terminal? So she decided to enjoy it, there in their little oasis in Newark, New Jersey.

As she walked through the little airport in Ithaca—Tompkins County Regional—she couldn't help but notice how tiny it was compared to Newark. But she loved it. It was so comfortable. She'd been at Cornell for five years now, and it felt like home. She'd been afraid she'd feel isolated out in the country, after growing up in the suburbs and living in cities all her adult life. But the university setting suited her well, and she was happy.

She found her car out in the parking lot, just where she'd left it. She squeezed her hand into the front pocket of her jeans, and pulled out her keys. Her car was a bit of a wreck, a twenty-year old brown Corolla with rust eating the lower quarter panels and door bottoms. The trunk creaked when she opened it, and the car bounced and creaked again when she dropped in her suitcase.

It was mid-September, and it was starting to get cold out, and she hoped the car would last another winter. She still didn't have the patience to let it warm up and had it out on the road within a minute of starting it.

She turned the radio on but then quickly turned it off, relishing the quiet. She thought about him on the way home. He was probably a cad. With those blue eyes. And he was so tall! She was almost 5'9 herself but had to crane her neck to look him in the eye when they were face-to-face.

But it was a welcome distraction. She had two classes to teach tomorrow, and even though she was well-prepared, it took a lot of energy out of her, and she was already dead tired. And to make it worse, they were total opposites: Introductory French with sixty-three students and a graduate seminar on nineteenth-century French literature with four students. She thought about stopping at the Indian take-out on Stewart Street but decided she would just have a cheese sandwich when she got home, suddenly very hungry.

As she turned down East Seneca, away from the school, she looked forward to her simple dinner, a little Balzac, and an early night. The clock was broken in her car, so she glanced at her watch. It was only eight, and she let out a little laugh. "Already!" saying to herself.

She was about to pull her car up the driveway, but it was blocked. A blue Honda. Jean. Her roommate. Well, not exactly her roommate. Vicky owned the house and rented out an upstairs room. She had a graduate student there last year. Tom. Also from the French Department. Nice, quiet, and he paid the rent on time. He was even a good conversationalist. But he was off to Stanford for the year, so now she had Jean, a senior majoring in economics. And what a pain she was. Never on time with the rent, and Vicky always had to ask for it. And she always seemed to leave her dirty dishes in the sink or out on the table. And—most horrifying of all—she, or one of her friends, would pee on the toilet seat in the downstairs powder room.

Vicky wasn't the kind to call her out on these things. Far too embarrassing. And uncivilized. She'd be gone at the end of the year. Then she'd find someone else. If she was still there. Tenure. She figured her odds were about 50-50. Either way, she'd know by the end of the year. Then there was the dictionary project. Bill—Professor William G. Elbaum—her advisor at Georgetown, was the project's founder and was still running it almost forty years later. He was eighty-eight and seemed to be going strong, but he was going to have to turn the reins over to someone before long, and she was the logical candidate. But nothing was guaranteed, and that new girl, Evelyn, was making inroads. And there were a couple of other former students to worry about too.

She finished parking the car out front, already annoyed at Jean, who was not supposed to park in the driveway, as she took her suitcase out of the trunk. A squeak and a slam later, she pulled up the handle, lifted it over the curb, and was pulling her purple carry-on up to the steps.

She dragged it up over the poured concrete steps, cracked with moss and other sprouts popping through the fissures, dating, no doubt from when the house was built, back in 1910. It wasn't a particularly nice house—wood-shingled in pale yellow, not quite Victorian and badly in need of renovation—but it was big with a full dining room, a parlor, and four bedrooms upstairs, although there was only the one full bath and that tiny powder room on the first floor.

She could see through the huge cut-glass window in the front door that the lights were out. Maybe Jean was out. Her car was there, but she might have walked to the library. She popped the door open and turned on the lights. The door was wide and heavy and rattled a little when she closed it. Everything seemed so ancient in the house, even compared to her parents' mid-century split-level.

She wheeled her suitcase over to the foot of the stairs and slipped into the powder room. It was tiny—barely the size of a closet—tucked neatly under the stairs. The seat was clean and even down. Hooray! When she finished, she washed her hands in the tiny, hundred-year-old, dual-spigot corner sink, her elbow hitting the wall as she dried her hands.

That cheese sandwich at last. But the bread—*her* bread—was half gone and left open. Stale. No matter. She'd toast it. She opened the fridge to get the cheese, but that was just simply gone. She was so annoyed that she threw the bread out, then took it out of the garbage, taped a piece of paper to it, and wrote a note. *Buy your own fucking bread and cheese,* she felt like writing, but she didn't. *Please replace what you use.* It sounded so lame. And besides, she'd lost her appetite. So the bread went back in the garbage, and she went upstairs to her room.

By the time she was in her nightshirt and socks, she was ready for Balzac, but she was too tired and drifted off to sleep. Then she thought of him again. Nick. No, Nicholas. She never got his last name. An engineer. Tall and handsome. And those blue eyes.

Her French class was in rare form the next morning. Cornell had beaten Harvard on a field goal in overtime, and the mood on campus was practically giddy. At least in French 112. There were a couple of football players in class, including the kid who'd made the winning kick—a 37-yarder. It started with a joke about "cut the grass" being translated as "mow ze lawn" in French and devolved from there.

She had to admit, it was funny. Ridiculous, but funny. So she laughed. She knew she had a goofy laugh, but it caught the class by surprise. They were already laughing, but it made them laugh even harder. And that made her laugh even harder. Then she asked the class, dead serious, if they knew that there was a special way in French to say "kick a football?" They paused for a second, unsure, before she delivered the punch line with perfect comedic timing: "punt le ball."

The air was still for a moment before one person then another then the whole class started cracking up. Their frumpy old professor with the gold-rimmed glasses had a sense of humor.

By this time, she was sitting on the desk in front of the class in the large lecture hall. It was five minutes before the bell, and she knew they weren't going to get any more work done, so she let them out early.

It was the graduate seminar that was death. Normally, that was her fun class to teach. Everyone wanted to be there, and it was nice to speak in real French. But there was one guy, *Guy*, ironically enough, who had to chime in with some inane remark on everything. And today, he was in rare form.

He was a half-black, French Canadian, who she actually liked. But he was trying too hard. And that accent. She could never get used to it. He spoke so slowly. "But don't you think Fréchette, at least, was the equivalent of de Maupassant?"

No. No I don't, she wanted to tell him. *I hate all of the French-Canadian writers.* But she didn't say it. The truth was, she'd never even heard of Fréchette. Some obscure hack from Quebec, no doubt. She didn't say that either. "It's all a matter of opinion," she told him. "Now let's stay focused. What has so captured the international audience about de Maupassant's stories?"

Normally, she'd have Thérèse in class to help her out, but she was absent that day. So it was just Guy, Darla, and Sandi. She could see that the other two were about as unamused as she was but unwilling or unable to stop it.

Then, just as he mentioned another forgotten Canuck, the bell rang, and she was free.

She met her friend Giselle, who was a Rumi scholar, from the Persian section of the Department of Near Eastern Studies, for lunch at Eddie's, a local sandwich shop downtown. She'd been dying to talk to her since her plane landed and barely waited for the poor woman to take her first bite of her tuna sub.

"I swear, maybe I'm being paranoid, but I think he's going to give it to Evelyn."

Giselle rushed her chewing and swallowed. "Relax, you're his girl." She looked her in the eye. "You're like the best graduate student he ever had."

She looked across at her, petite, brown-skinned, with short black hair. She first met Giselle when they were both undergraduates at Georgetown. Then, later, both with their respective PhDs in hand, they ran into each other again at Columbia, when they were both post docs. Now, here they were, both at Cornell. But Giselle had tenure, and Vicky, well, she was just waiting to come out the other side. "I know. But he gives me a ridiculous amount of work to do. I have a pile of entries I have to finish by Monday. Doesn't he know I have classes to teach up here?"

Giselle laughed and finished another bite, a little less harried. "You mean your old thesis advisor uses you like slave labor?"

Vicky laughed, and Giselle gestured to her plate. "Come on, eat your sandwich."

She had forgotten how hungry she was, so she picked up her sandwich and dug in. A ham and brie panini. It seemed a little out of place for a joint like Eddie's, but this was a university town, and they had to cater to a diverse crowd. She savored the first bite and washed it down with a gulp of Diet Pepsi. Then another.

"Don't worry, it'll all work out." Giselle told her. "You'll get the dictionary project, and you'll get tenure."

Smart and together, she had a calming voice. Vicky didn't know how she did it: Gotten tenure and published two books, all while going through a horrible divorce. They never really talked about it—it happened just when she got to Columbia—but it was just as well: she wasn't good at giving advice about stuff like that anyway.

So they talked about the football game and a couple of poems Giselle was working on, and they finished their lunch. Vicky spent the weekend working on the dictionary and relaxing with a few black-and-white films from the French New Wave, starting with *A Man and a Woman.* She'd lectured on Lelouch back at Columbia, and had fallen in love with his films.

It was hot in Miami. Even in the hallway of a luxury building like his. Even in September. He couldn't wait for that cool rush of air conditioning when he opened the door. He pulled out his keys, still holding his suitcase and still thinking about Colón. He'd asked him to meet him at the airport, drive back with him to his condo downtown so they could talk in the car. He figured that was safe.

He told him about the house up in Albany, how it didn't look like they were cutting any corners, how everything seemed strangely normal. But Colón didn't seem bothered by it. That big black moustache hardly seemed to move. "Don't worry about it, Nicholas," he told him. "Just pick up your envelope tomorrow from Badillos."

And that told him that there was something to worry about. But what could he say? "Yeah, sure. No problem." And the conversation seemed to end there.

So he'd pick up the envelope from Badillos at the shop in Little Havana on Friday morning. Another $5,000, though he never bothered to count it. Then he'd relax for the weekend and head back up on Monday to do it all over again.

He popped the door open and stepped into that cool wave. Relief.

It was broken by the sight of his wife in a bikini out on the balcony lying on a recliner. It was dusk, and the image was striking, there on the 23rd floor over-looking Miami Beach, the outline of her legs against the darkening sky and the glass rail. He could just make out her smooth, flat stomach. She had a hell of a body, that was for sure. Especially for a fifty-two-year-old.

She picked up her drink from the side table, sipping it through a straw, when he closed the door, and she turned and caught sight of him. She swiveled around on her butt and stood, pinning on a big smile, still holding her drink. She opened the door and stepped inside the apartment, still smiling and tilting her glass. "Want a piña colada?"

He popped on the lights and looked at her. He could see the flaws now, the winkles around her eyes, the slight sag in her skin, but he didn't care. He was still wound up from the woman in the airport and the trip up north and that talk with Colón. He wanted her, right there, and he knew she'd let him, but he'd take it slow, make it last all night, and they'd both wake up in the morning, her with those dreamy brown eyes, and him with a pit of regret. But right then, it was what he needed.

"Sure."

So she poured him one and then another. And they ordered take-out from the rib place down Biscayne Boulevard, and she ended up licking sauce off his face, still in her bikini, until she took it off.

And the next morning, there he was, in that bright, white bedroom, staring at those big brown eyes. But he surprised himself and took her again.

They stayed in bed half the weekend, only going out for a nice dinner on Sunday night. And, of course, him going out alone, to the shop in Little Havana to get that envelope. Badillos wasn't even there, with his sagging face and that gold tooth. But the envelope was, and that was all that counted. Still, he wondered.

Then he was off to Albany again. He'd almost forgotten about his date with Vicky. Vicky Scardo, with the gold-rimmed glasses and the purple suitcase.

When his plane landed, he wondered if he'd have trouble finding her. Or if she'd even remember that they had a date. He didn't see her. So he went to the bar and had his usual. An hour later, and he was still there. So he figured that was it. And then he saw her.

She was wearing a black pantsuit, and she looked good, still towing that purple carry-on. She saw him, smiled and waved, taking the barstool next to him and slipping her purse off her shoulder.

"Sorry I'm late," she said. "Mechanical trouble in Ithaca." She rolled her eyes, all dramatic-like. "I was afraid I wasn't going to make it!" Then she broke out in a big smile.

"Well, I have a place all picked out," he said. "Unless you want a drink first."

"No, no," she said. "Let's go, have dinner."

He signaled Ralph, whom he could see with the Mona Lisa smile of a student of the human condition, having played some small role in connecting two people, even in this most unlikely setting. Nicholas left him another ten, and they were off.

He'd found a little French restaurant up the adjacent corridor. It was an outpost of a bigger place across in Manhattan, but, he guessed, with a more limited menu. But maybe, he hoped, the same class and intimacy.

"Sure I know Maurice's!" she said, as the waiter seated them. "I used to live in the City, you know," she added, fun and playful.

And they talked and ate.

It turned out they both liked Jazz. Al Jarreau and Dave Brubeck. And she knew more about sports than he would have expected—her dad was a huge Redskins fan and used to be a season ticket holder to the Orioles. "Well, actually, it belonged to all the guys at work," she told him. "But my dad used to organize it all." Then she paused and seemed to look right at him. "He was a cop. A detective, actually," she said, as if to apologize for her blue-collar origins. But he hardly noticed, frozen in place, a shiver running up his spine like she knew something about him that he didn't want her to.

"Is that right?" he said, hoping she wouldn't notice.

"Yeah, gold shield," she told him, proud and oblivious behind those thick glasses.

Then they had dessert, and it was over.

"This was too short!" she told him.

"Yeah," he said, thinking it was one of the best dates he'd ever had.

"Well, we'll have to pick it up on Thursday," she said, beaming, liked *she'd* tricked *him* into it this time. And he smiled back.

"It's a date. But only if you give me your number."

So they exchanged info. She stared at his name. Nicholas Barczynski. "Wow! That's some last name!" Then she looked at him. "How do you pronounce that?"

"Bar-CHIN-ski," he said. "It's Polish," he added with a grin.

And she repeated it. "Nicholas Barczynski." Then she paused as if to savor each syllable. "I like it. I like it a lot." And he knew that that meant *him,* that she liked *him* a lot.

So he asked her on another date. Thursday, during their next layover. There in Terminal C.

And that's how it started in earnest. Every Monday and Thursday. Dinner there in Terminal C. There were other restaurants, and they tried several. An Italian place called *Ponte Vecchio,* another French place, a bistro called *Michelle's,* and a burger joint with artisanal buns and toppings.

They ate and talked and smiled into each other's eyes. They watched the Skins and the Dolphins at Lombardi's Sports Bar, and he teased her when the Dolphins won in a blowout. He learned that she was equal parts Italian, French, and Greek, and he realized that he could see it in her eyes and the angles of her face: the stern goddess and the warm wise eyes and the soft wild curves that he wanted with an ever greater hunger.

Then they started to text each other. At first, it was just to tell the other person that there was a delay or a change in plans. Then, one day, he called. She was sitting in her office at the French Academy in Washington, and she told him she'd call back later, but they ended up talking for twenty minutes anyway.

"There are supposed to be thunderstorms this afternoon," he said. "All up and down the east coast."

The sky was clear, and she hadn't heard anything. She hadn't even been on the internet to check her email or the news. She was sitting, dressed in a nice skirt and pantyhose, coming off an early morning meeting with the institute's director and her former advisor, Elbaum, the head of the dictionary project. That she was the only one asked along lifted her spirits, and she went back to her office on the fourth floor, there on G Street, to finish the section she was working on before heading back to her parents' place on the other side of the border in Maryland to change her clothes, grab her suitcase, and say a quick goodbye.

She was getting ready to leave when he called. Now she was late, but she didn't want to hang up. So they talked for another five minutes, until he, finally, had to go. She suddenly felt very close to him and wanted to tell him, tell him something, but she settled for a simple "See you later, I hope." She could've kicked herself. But there was no time. She saved her work on the server, grabbed her coat and bag, and headed out to hail a taxi.

By the time she got to her parents' house, she was running a good forty-five minutes late. There was no time to change. She hurried through the front door and headed up the short staircase of the three-bed split-level.

"Hi Mom!" she said, not even stopping. "I'm running late."

"Do you want something to eat?"

"No," she yelled from the bedroom, emerging a few seconds later with her suitcase in tow. "The cab is waiting. Where is Dad?"

"In the den, watching TV."

He was always in the den watching TV, but she always asked. She left her suitcase by the front door and went through the kitchen out the other side to the den. A gray-haired man with a moustache looked back over his shoulder and smiled as she came around leaned in and kissed him on the cheek. "I've got to go. I'll be back next week. I love you." Then she hugged him there in his chair, straightened up, kissed and hugged her mother, and headed back through the house, almost forgetting her suitcase on the way out.

By the time she got to Newark, she was wondering what all the fuss had been about. The skies were still clear. Then it came: torrential rain. And thunder and lightning. Planes were still landing, but only a few and nothing from Albany, even though the board said his plane should have landed fifteen minutes ago.

The board updated: DELAYED—another thirty minutes. Then forty-five. Then, finally, with that worry working its way through the pit of her stomach, she watched the little propeller plane, bucked by the wind, touch down, a spray of water coming off the runway filtered through that ever-changing pattern of drops on the large glass windows of the terminal.

He had to come through the rain on the runway to get to the gate, and she spotted him out there, her heart beating with anticipation and just a little fear, as she watched a hard strike then another off in the distance.

She spotted him out there—6'4 with his long black coat and black briefcase. He'd told her he always sent his bag through—too much trouble to lug it around for three hours—but the briefcase had his most important papers, and he couldn't afford to lose it.

When he stepped through the gate and into the terminal, she came up to him and hugged him, even though he was wet.

"Glad you could make it."

There was an instant, an odd little fleck of time, when she thought they would kiss, but it passed, and that momentary look of astonishment that she thought she saw on his face broke into that big toothy smile. "You know I always keep our dates."

Then she realized that she was holding his hands, even the one with the briefcase, and she let go. And they walked together into the terminal until he headed to the men's room to clean up, and she went over to *Michelle's* to get them a table.

They watched the board as they ate. By the time they were done, it had turned from a sea of delayed flights to "All flights postponed until further notice." Nobody seemed to know when it would let up. A couple of hours? All afternoon? Who could say? But everyone realized it could be a long afternoon. "Don't leave the terminal," the woman on the PA announced. So they sat and talked, shared dessert and had an after-dinner drink and then another. She had Amaretto, and he had Sambuca. Then, with a line of people piling up to get a table, they left and went back to the terminal and sat hip-to-hip in the row of chairs at her gate.

She was feeling drowsy and fell asleep on his shoulder. Then she woke up a few minutes later, startled at having taken the liberty, but he put his arm around her and gently pushed her head back down. "It's ok. Rest. It's been a long day."

And it made her feel warm and cared for, so she closed her eyes. But the rush of his arm around her and his hand on her side just above her hip, giving a gentle caress, kept her awake. And she looked up at him, still on his shoulder, and started to talk.

"There are things about me you don't know," she told him. None of it mattered before, but now, all of a sudden, it did. So she told him. Everything. There on a row of seats at gate 31B, snuggling into his chest, feeling his hand, strong but gentle, looking up at those concerned eyes.

She told him about her first time, when she was seventeen. "He was an older man," she said. "And I had a terrible crush on him." She was leaning on Nicholas now, her shoulder against his arm, his hand on her opposite shoulder. "So I asked him upstairs in my parents' house to show him my collection of porcelain dolls, and we kissed." Then she continued with some difficulty. "My parents were out, and we went into my bedroom. And it just got out of hand. I really didn't want to go that far, and I tried to stop him." She felt Nicholas tense like a board.

"Are you saying he raped you?"

She looked up at him, virile and feral, and it made her feel alarmed and protected at the same time. "Well, yes, technically, but it just got out of hand, that's all. He didn't hit me or hurt me, and I wasn't screaming or anything." And she couldn't believe what she was saying, with her Ivy League feminist credentials screaming to get out. But this wasn't the tenure committee, and she didn't care.

It seemed to work. She felt his body relax a little, though she didn't have the nerve to look him in the eye. Then she told him the rest. "He was my dad's partner." She could practically feel him shudder. "I've never told anyone. You're the first." And he seemed to sense that this wasn't about him; that she was pouring her soul out to him, and he just needed to listen.

Then she told him everything. That she'd never been able to have a real relationship after that. That she'd decided at one point that she was a lesbian and had a short affair with a female graduate student when she was a post doc at Columbia. And how it "felt like nothing" to her, that even the couple of times they'd had sex "felt like a gynecological exam." Then she looked up at him and smirked. "You're shocked."

But he looked straight at her. "You're an amazing person."

It caught her off guard, and she reached up and kissed him, and, for the first time in a very long time, she felt something, something strong and real, and she wanted to tell him, but she didn't dare.

"Wow," she said, nestling back down in his chest, feet up, lying across three seats with their armrests up, her own arms folded over her chest.

She could hear his heart beating, and it made her want more, but they were in the middle of an airport, lit golden against the black sky of a storm, and she couldn't. So she told him the rest, about the only other relationship she'd had.

It had lasted five years and ended only a few years ago. He was twenty-five years older than she, another French scholar, who had published a seminal article on the influences of Late Church Latin on the sociolinguistics of the French language and nothing of any importance since. Half academic celebrity and half pariah, she'd met him at a conference at the University of Arizona, and they hit it off.

He was a Vietnam vet, like her dad, who came back, got his PhD at Michigan, published his famous article, and landed at Duke. By the time they wanted to unload him, he already had tenure, and it was too late.

She connected to the pathos in him, instinctively knowing that there was more. And there was. He had been wounded in a firefight in the Mekong Delta in 1965, and although, by all outward appearances, he had made a complete recovery, the injury had rendered him completely impotent, destroying all desire and the ability to have children along with it. No one knew. It explained why he had never married, and why he felt so safe to her.

She never told a soul, and they enjoyed their sexless, mostly long-distance relationship. He even managed to arrange a sabbatical at Cornell and trips to Washington to see her. She loved his mind, his quiet, wounded soul, and his vulnerability. But then, just as it was becoming clear that it was not enough, his dark side, frustrated and tortured, began to emerge. A permanent chip on his shoulder. Unable to make love; unable to publish. Comfortable, but aging. An increasing liability to the institution supporting him and the woman he was involved with. It ended with a whimper, and she didn't regret it.

"After that, I just figured I was as asexual as he was, and that I should be concentrating my life on my work." But now she wasn't so sure. There was a man, still married to be sure, but lying right under her nose, as it were, all 6′4 of him.

Then she fell asleep, and when he woke her up, the storm had cleared.

"Your flight is boarding soon," he told her, looking down into her eyes, stroking her hair.

She was curled up, asleep in his lap. It was light out now, but she could barely make out his face, Her glasses, gone. And then he handed them to her, and she sat up and put them on. She wasn't sure how long she'd slept for, but she wanted more. In his lap, with his arm around her. But there was no time. She needed to go to the bathroom too, but she'd wait for the plane.

They started boarding a minute later, and she kissed him goodbye. It was short but deep, and she could taste him, the sweetness against the stubble. She wanted more, and she knew he did too, and it made her smile. "I'll see you Monday," she said. Then a simple "Bye." She knew he was watching her, but she didn't mind. Then she entered the plane, and she was alone.

He still had an hour until his flight was leaving, and he went back to the food court for some breakfast. His head was spinning. Delicate and complex, smart and impassioned. She was fantastic. He thought of her walking onto that plane, pushing her hair back, wiggling in that skirt. He decided she was the prettiest thing he'd ever seen.

He couldn't get her out of his head. He decided he wasn't hungry. He'd sit and relax. He'd been up all night, stroking her hair, feeling her on his body, almost going out of his mind at times. But he was too excited, too restless to sit. He had that feeling, warm and fuzzy, like when he kissed Jen Wilson in high school then touched her ass, and she'd let him. And he knew now like he'd known then: He had a girlfriend. The trouble was, he still had a wife.

He'd worry about it later. For now, he'd walk around the airport thinking about her, wondering if she was sleeping on the plane or thinking about him too. He'd call her later, see how she was doing. Or maybe he should let her sleep. Then he realized, he *was* actually hungry, and he circled back to the food court and got a breakfast burrito at *La Pequeña Cantina*.

His plane still delayed, an hour later, he was at the bar, having a drink, and chatting with Ralph. He was also from Newark, born and bred. His father owned a bar in the Ironbound but lost it when he pissed off the wrong hood. They both laughed. *Sounds about right.* Then his boarding call finally came, and he headed out.

There were two pings on his phone on the way to the gate. Vicky he figured, pulling it from his pocket. *Back in Ithaca safe and sound. Can't wait to see you Monday. Hope you're not scared off! :-)*

But the second one was from his wife: *Miss you.*

Two women in two cities, and him halfway in between, in Newark, New Jersey, the Brick City, the city of his birth, getting on a plane. As he took his seat, he knew he'd have to choose but not today. Today it was enough to savor it, letting that second shot of Johnnie Walker Red work its magic, thinking about it all and smiling to himself as he leaned back and closed his eyes.

A while later, he was back in Miami. It didn't take long for the phone to ring. Colón.

"I think our boy Jimmy's going off the reservation."

He didn't know exactly what that meant, but he wasn't going to ask. Colón wouldn't tell him anyway. "What do you want me to do?" he said, almost defensive.

"Be careful."

And then he hung up.

It was all too much. By the time he opened his apartment door, he was ready to collapse into bed. He entered, praying his wife wasn't there, and she wasn't. So he took off his clothes, went to the bathroom, brushed his teeth, and went to bed.

Six hours later he woke up. His wife was still out, so he took a shower, and when he came out to get dressed, there she was, tight stare, arms folded.

"So, what's her name?"

"Who?" he asked, taking off the towel and putting on underwear.

"The bitch that you're fucking up in Albany or wherever the fuck you go every week."

He could see her eyes turning red, and he suddenly felt tired and awful. *I'm not fucking her,* he wanted to say. *And how the hell did you figure out that I was seeing someone anyway?*

Then he thought to deny it, but he'd never get away with it. So he decided to come clean. They were supposed to be getting divorced anyway, so what was the difference?

But she pounced before he had a chance to even answer. "You son of a bitch! I hate you!" She pounded on his chest, him there in his white briefs.

"You're out of your mind." was all he could manage as he struggled to get dressed, until he left the apartment.

Walking around, he realized that she had probably gone through his phone, seen the texts. Maybe she even smelled her on his clothes. She was sharp like that. So he went back home and talked to her.

She was dry-eyed but impassioned when she told him that she still loved him. But the tears started flowing when she recounted how they'd made love all weekend long when he was seeing someone on the side. And he told her he loved her too, but that he *was* seeing someone but that their marriage was supposed to be over and he needed time to think.

"You still love me?" she said, that seeming to be all she heard.

"Yes," he said, even though he shouldn't have, because he needed time to think.

Then she looked at him, and he thought she might try to lead him into the bedroom, but she didn't, and he knew she was afraid that he might not go, even though he probably would have.

They barely talked all weekend. He went to Little Havana and got his envelope from Badillos. And then he went to the movies alone to clear his head. He figured he'd have dinner with her on Sunday night, but she was out with her friends. And then it was Monday, and he was headed back to Albany.

He hadn't gotten a chance to call Vicky all weekend and hadn't even texted. And he realized: she hadn't either. But he was still looking forward to seeing her. More than ever.

Then he got off the plane at Terminal C and saw that her flight had been delayed—first forty-five minutes, then ninety, then three hours, and he realized he wasn't going to get to see her. He wondered if fate was intervening. Thanksgiving was next week, and then they would be in the home stretch until Christmas. His routine would continue with hardly a break, but she would be off for almost a month. Maybe that thunderstorm was the high point, and that was it. Then his phone rang.

"I miss you," she said.

"I miss you too."

She told him how busy she'd been but that she was hoping he'd call, and when he didn't she'd felt awful, but at least she'd get to see him soon, but now here she was stranded on the runway in Ithaca.

So he told her about the fight he'd had with his wife and how tense things were and then he said it, "I think I'm falling in love with you."

And her voice broke with excitement. "Me too!"

And they talked almost the whole time until his plane took off.

When he landed in Albany, his phone rang. It was his wife. He let it go through to voicemail. He slept like a rock at the Motel 6 and didn't even stop to listen to her voice message. Then a ping—a text from Vicky: *Still feel the same?*

She was like a high school kid. *Yes,* he texted back, and she sent him three smiley faces and an XOXO.

And then, like none of it had ever happened, he was back at Jimmy's Diner in Utica.

He walked in and gave Jo Jo the briefcase. But this time, he stopped Nicholas and frisked him.

Nicholas looked over at Jimmy. "What the fuck is this?"

Jimmy was sorting a deck of cards in front of a half-eaten breakfast of steak and eggs and answered without even looking up. "New procedure."

So the goon went up and down, under his arms and up his legs. When he got to his crotch, he squeezed until it hurt, and Nicholas pulled away. The man laughed, then looked over at Jimmy. "He's clean."

Nicholas had thought about carrying a gun but just then, he was glad he didn't have one. Somebody would have ended up dead. So he let it go and walked over to sit with Jimmy.

"That's bullshit," he said.

Jimmy looked up at him, finally. "You think so? Then tell those Spics down in Miami to cool it."

Nicholas had no clue what Jimmy was talking about, but he was getting the creeping feeling that it was all about to blow up, and he was going to be caught right in the middle. "I'll pass the message along."

"Good, you do that."

Linda the waitress was there as usual, but he didn't order anything this time, while he waited for the people in the back to count the money. When the man stuck his hand out and gave the ok signal to Jimmy, Jimmy tilted his head at Nicholas, and Nicholas got up to leave.

Jo Jo was half-blocking the exit, sitting on the edge of the booth with his legs sticking out. But Nicholas didn't react, reaching down to grab the empty brief-case and move around him. Then he stood, blocking Nicholas completely, there towering over him, crouched with his left hand grabbing the handle of the briefcase. It happened fast.

Like an old third baseman, Nicholas threw his right hand up into his crotch and squeezed as hard as he could, rising and lifting him up until he flipped him back up onto the table which collapsed under his weight. He was almost as tall as Nicholas and at least a hundred pounds heavier, but he was whimpering like a baby. "The way you touched me before, I thought you wanted to be my girlfriend. Is that what you want?"

The man cried out.

"I can't hear you. Was that a yes?"

"No!"

Then another thug came to blindside him, but he was too fast, slamming him in the head with the empty briefcase just as he let go of Jo Jo's crotch.

Jimmy looked up at the scene, unperturbed. The other two thugs in the place were ready to pounce. Nicholas was being tested and he knew it. Then Jimmy put his hand up to stop them as he looked over at Nicholas. "You move well for a big man. Maybe I'll hire you."

"No thanks," he said. Then, looking around, "Utica's way too much of a shithole for me."

Jimmy's face fell, and he knew he'd stepped in it, gone too far, but it was the adrenaline talking.

"Suit yourself. But who's going to pay for my table?"

Nicholas straightened his tie and took the briefcase, turning back and gesturing to Jo Jo still writhing with his hands on his crotch. "Why don't you ask him? He's the one who broke it."

Nicholas was a bundle of nerves for the rest of the day, although that adrenaline high wasn't entirely unpleasant. He figured he'd passed the test, but he also knew it wouldn't be long before it all came apart.

He went to his appointments, wrote his reports, and told Colón what happened as soon as he got back to Miami.

"I want out," Nicholas told him, but Colón could be persuasive. So Nicholas agreed to continue.

He told him what he already knew: That Jimmy was testing him, that he was just a cog in the works, not worth killing, since it could screw up the whole operation. And that was exactly why he couldn't replace him now. Then, finally, "Don't worry, I'll take care of Jimmy. You just do your bit." Nicholas looked at those black eyes and that moustache across from him in the car. A man to be reckoned with for sure. So he agreed. "Okay," he told him. "No problem." But he felt himself sinking like a man in quicksand.

The next few weeks were a blur. Up and back, with drops to Jimmy and reports to Gorman. Jo Jo was gone, and it was like the whole thing never happened. But he knew it had. He knew Jimmy was biding his time, that it would all explode, probably sooner than later. He just didn't want to get caught in the middle.

Even with the danger, he could hardly focus. It all seemed like empty time, time to kill, waiting to see or talk to Vicky. Then, suddenly, they'd be together, and all the rest of it—the money, the thugs, his wife—would fade into oblivion. They were like teenagers, the two of them. They would walk in the airport, holding hands, kissing and hugging when they would first see each other and when they would part. He told her about trying out for the Tigers and why he loved engineering and where to get great Portuguese food in Newark. And she told him about her trips to France and working on the dictionary, and what it was like to be a cop's daughter from Maryland.

They began to talk and text every day when they were apart and ended up on the phone together for over three hours on Thanksgiving Day. She was with her parents in DC, and he was with his wife. They'd had a fight, and she stormed out, so he called Vicky.

She seemed to sense that he was a bit off, but a lot of people are like that on the holidays, and she didn't seem to think much of it. "I was alone last year," she told him. "I drank a whole bottle of wine. Chardonnay. Really expensive. I was sick as a dog."

"Well, you're not alone now," he told her.

There was a pause on the other end of the line. "You're a sweet man."

Then he asked her what she was wearing.

"A white dress," she told him. "It's sort of a tradition of mine to wear all white on Thanksgiving."

"Everything white?" he asked with a hint of mischief.

"Yes," she said, amused at his interest. "White everything."

Whenever he'd talk to her on the phone after that, he'd always ask her what color underwear she was wearing, and she'd tell him, and it would drive him crazy. Then they'd see each other, and he wanted to make love to her, and she wanted to let him, but there was no place. It was part of what had made the whole thing safe, their world there in Terminal C, but it had become their prison.

There was still his wife and Jimmy and Colón and those damn houses in Albany. He just wished it would end. So he decided to enjoy his escapes, even if they did leave him increasingly frustrated.

They celebrated her birthday—December 16th— at the bar. Ralph got them a piece of cake with a candle, and he gave her an expensive necklace, amethyst and tanzanite in a white gold setting, and she practically swooned. When she put it on, she turned and knocked over his briefcase. It hit the ground with a hollow thud, and she looked at him puzzled, but he looked up and started talking about the necklace again before she had a chance to say anything, and the moment passed.

Later, at the gate, she sat in his lap and told him that she loved him, the small inconsistency forgotten or forgiven. But he was thinking of his wife, and couldn't say it back, and she didn't ask him to.

"I need to think," he told her, and she knew. He had a wife.

So she nodded and got up from his lap, gave him a small peck on the cheek, and walked onto her plane.

He watched her, sad and uncertain, thinking about it all the way to Miami.

When he got to the condo, his wife was in rare form. Already tipsy, eyes red from crying, and wearing nothing but a pair of red panties, she still managed a smile at him. She seemed to be offering herself to him, almost desperate, and it made it hard for him to think.

So he asked her to get dressed, and she did. Then he told her everything. "Her name is Vicky," he started. "I know," she said. And he told her how they'd met, and that nothing, really, had happened yet, and that he needed time to think. "Ok," she told him. And then it was time to head back north.

He hadn't talked to Vicky all weekend. It was too much. But then, there in Miami Airport, he called her.

"Hi," he said.

"Hi."

"It's snowing in Boston," he said, trying to keep it safe.

"Yeah, but it's supposed to blow out to sea," she told him.

There was a pause, then he said it, "I love you, Vicky."

There was another pause, and then he could hear that she was crying. Just a little. They were happy tears, but she was trying to hide them.

"Are you still there?" he asked.

"Yes, yes, I'm still here!" she said.

"Well, what are you thinking?"

"It's about time!"

And they both laughed.

By the time he landed in Newark, it was snowing hard. The forecast had been wrong: The cold front had shifted south, pushed by an Arctic air mass that was now colliding with warmer air coming up the Atlantic coast to produce a severe Nor'easter. He wondered if she'd make it, as he trudged through the snow on the runway, clutching that briefcase, feeling the wet seep into his shoes.

Her flight was listed as on-time, but he didn't believe it. He headed to the bar when his phone rang. Colón.

"Nothing to worry about," he said, which probably meant there was. "But Jo Jo's dead. They found him washed up on the Brooklyn piers."

"Is that right?" he said, trying to sound normal in the airport crowd. He knew enough not to ask any questions, like who whacked him. He didn't need to know. It could have been the boys from Miami or maybe Jimmy finally got noticed downstate, and they took out one of his boys and were sending him a message. Or maybe Jimmy was just doing some housecleaning of his own. Any way you'd slice it, it was trouble for Nicholas.

Then, still on the phone, he ran straight into Vicky. The conversation was over anyway, and Colón hung up.

She hugged and kissed him, and it felt great. Then she pulled back and smiled, almost mischievous. "Who was that?"

"Business call," he told her, and that was the end of it.

She kissed him again and asked where they were going for dinner, and he told her Michelle's. Looking out the windows, he got a funny feeling. There was nothing but white by now. He couldn't even see the runway. So on the way over, he went to the men's room and made a quick phone call before meeting her there. There was already a huge line, and they realized they'd never get in. Then came the announcement: All flights cancelled for the next 24 hours.

She looked at him, more amused than troubled, still holding his hand. "What are we going to do?"

He grinned. "Well, there's no point sleeping in the airport." Then he grinned wider and gestured with his thumb over his shoulder. "There's a Marriot here at the airport. Really nice. I used to carry bags there when I was a kid." He didn't tell her his father had been head porter, but he wasn't sure she would have heard him anyway.

The flash of excitement crossed her face, and then she saw everyone suddenly on their phones trying to make arrangements. "Hurry up!" she said, smiling and excited. "Before all the rooms are gone!"

But he just kept grinning at her. "It's all taken care of. Best suite in the house." He'd called, he told her, when he slipped off to the men's room. He still had a few contacts there, which was true, and called in an old favor. On top of beating the rush. "The shuttle leaves every ten minutes."

She jumped into his arms, and he thought he was going to explode. As they sat in the shuttle, they decided they'd have dinner first in the restaurant over at the hotel. Once they were up in the room, he knew it would never happen.

Vicky went off to the bathroom, as the bellboy off-loaded her purple carry-on. As Nicholas reached for his wallet, he realized he hadn't had a chance to stop at an ATM and had no cash on him.

"Just a minute," he told the bellboy, who stood there, hoping for his tip. "Can you wait for me in the hallway?"

"Yes, sir!"

And Nicholas did what he had never done before: He unlocked the briefcase and opened it, mid-trip. There was a gun in there now amidst the piles of 20s, and he thought how she could come back in at any moment as he fumbled to pull out a couple of hundred dollars that he'd put back later, when he could get to an ATM.

Then the kid walked back in, and he closed the briefcase, which was open facing away from his line of sight. He handed the kid a twenty, and the kid asked how much he wanted back. "Keep it," he told him, and the kid smiled for the first time. "Merry Christmas."

Just then, Vicky came back into the room.

"If you need anything, just call down at the front desk," the kid said, looking over at Vicky too. "Ask for Alejandro—Alex." He turned and left, and for the first time, they were alone.

The briefcase was on the bed, closed but with both latches open. He was about to grab it, snap the latches shut, roll the combo lock, and put it off in the corner, but she reached past him and grabbed it first, before he had a chance, picking it up off the bed and putting on the floor. All the while, she was giving him a warm, lascivious grin, broken for an instant by a quizzical look that he understood to be surprise at the briefcase's sudden heaviness. Whatever she was thinking about the briefcase, it didn't last long, and it didn't stop her. With the last obstacle out of the way, she pushed him back on the bed and kissed him.

She was inexperienced but had all the right instincts. She let him undress her, and he took her top and bra off first. Then she helped him take off her jeans. Then came his shirt and pants. He kissed her everywhere, and she whispered his name, telling him how much she loved him.

Then, when it was time, they took off the rest. Her, then him. She seemed surprised by what she saw, almost giggling with delight. It hurt her at first—she wasn't used to it—but it wasn't long before she wanted to do it again. There was a third time before morning, and when she woke up, she sat straight up in bed and looked right at him. "Wow!"

The snow had stopped, and the sky was clear. He could see the thick blanket of snow covering everything. They'd be on their way in a few hours probably.

But in the meantime, he was enjoying the most perfect moment of his life.

Leaning on one elbow, he looked at her, naked, there on the bed. She was forty-three now and curvy as hell with spectacular boobs and great muscle tone, all of it carefully hidden in a mousy college professor. "You're gorgeous," he told her, and he could see that she had let the rest of the world go and decided to believe him.

"You're pretty hot stuff yourself, Nicholas Barczynski!"

Then he kissed her and asked if she was hungry.

"Starving!" she told him.

"How about ordering us some breakfast while I take a quick shower?" he told her. "Unless you want to go first."

"No, you go," she told him. If only she hadn't.

He'd forgotten about his unlocked briefcase. By the time he came out, it was open on the desk. She was already dressed. She looked over at him. Anger, disgust, and even a little pity and shame.

He could see it all in her eyes. The cop's daughter, victimized again by another creep, a creep she trusted but shouldn't have.

"My plane is leaving in a little while. I'm going back over to the airport," she told him, matter-of-fact. "It would be good if you could stay here until my plane is gone."

He said nothing.

Then she grabbed her purple bag and went through the door, but not before she turned back and told him, "Don't ever contact me again."

The door slammed, and he went over and sat down on the bed, still wearing nothing but a towel, and stared at the open briefcase—empty on the way down, full, with $50,000 in cash and a gun on the way up. Every week. She was too smart not to put it together. A bag man. Nothing but a cheap criminal. Out of Miami. To god-know-who in Albany. He closed the briefcase and got dressed. Then his phone rang. Colón.

By the time he was on the New York Thruway, he was furious. At himself for not stopping at that ATM, for not letting her shower first so he could lock the briefcase, for the unkind hand of fate. Then he put it out of his mind. He had a delivery to make. In Utica. Colón had told him: They knew he was stuck in Newark, and it might be hours before his plane would leave. So they told him to rent a car and drive up, make the delivery that night. As if it wasn't dangerous enough in the daytime. Then Colón told him the rest.

He thought about his wife, but then he put her out of his mind too. There was a meeting in Utica and black ice all over the road, and he couldn't be late. He needed to focus.

When he pulled up to the diner, it was late—almost 11 pm. He noticed four or five cars still out on the street, but everything was closed, except Jimmy's. It was dim inside when he walked in, and he noticed a man, big, where Jo Jo used to be. Three other men sat with Jimmy. There was no room for him at the booth. That's when he knew.

"Give Teddy the briefcase," Jimmy said without even looking up. "If you're so much as twenty bucks short, I'll put one in your eye."

He'd forgotten, the ATM. But he knew they were going to kill him anyway. And then he realized, Jimmy killed Jo Jo. He'd caught him skimming, and he had him whacked. And somehow, they figured he was in on it. Colón had it right. Then he spotted him in the reflection off the glass out of the corner of his eye. The rest of it happened fast.

The big man came at him, hand out, and Nicholas turned like he was at bat and swung the briefcase up as hard as he could, catching him solid under the jaw. That's when the shooting started. Two guns pointed at him, firing, as he pulled the briefcase over like a shield. He could feel the thick stacks of money take the shots. Then shots over his shoulder and through the glass from the other side. Colón and his men.

Nicholas hit the deck, rolled to the side, and pulled his .38 from the small of his back. Two more men came from the back with shotguns. He shot one of them in the gut, and when the other went to return fire, he nailed him with a ten-ringer, killing him on the spot. Jimmy made a run for the door, but he never made it. There was blood everywhere, and he could hear Linda screaming. There were at least fifteen more shots. Then the lights went out.

When Vicky got to the airport, it all hit her like a safe being dropped on her head. She found her way to the bathroom, locked herself in a stall, and cried. She hated herself for it. "I'm so fucking stupid!" she said in a whisper. She was never going to tell anyone, that was for sure. Then she took a deep breath and pulled herself together. She'd forget about it, that's all. Sure, it would take a while, but what else could she do?

If her parents ever knew—her father—she felt so ashamed. And then, she realized, sore. They had screwed so much, and it had been such a long time, that she was actually sore. Chagrined, she laughed and shook her head. She couldn't wait to get out of Newark.

At the ticket counter, they told her there were no flights to DC—all cancelled until further notice. Even though it was now clear in Newark, the storm had made its way down south and settled over Washington, dumping over two feet, and it was still snowing. She realized that she was not going to make it down there this week.

"What do you have going back to Ithaca?"

The man behind the counter typed into the computer. He was young and thin with pale skin and stubble, but she could tell that he was honest and good at his job. Why couldn't she find someone like him?

He looked up, "There's one leaving in fifteen minutes. It's boarding now."

"You have room for one?"

Ninety minutes later, she was on the ground in Ithaca, and a half hour after that, she was back at her place, clearing her renter's pizza boxes then heading up to her room.

"Are you okay?"

She was surprised by the voice—Jen, her renter; she had thought she was alone. "Yeah, fine. I just got caught in the snowstorm and had to cancel my trip this week."

"You look like you're about to cry."

"I'm just tired."

Vicky turned to head up the stairs, and the voice called after her. "Sorry about the pizza boxes."

"It's okay."

"I would have cleaned them up, you know."

Halfway up the stairs, Vicky looked over at her and forced a smile. She knew that the girl could sense that something else was wrong, and that she was either being nosey or maybe she genuinely wanted to help. But Vicky was about to burst into tears and that would make it so much worse. So she smiled at her and said, "I know," and headed up to her room, locked the door, and burst into tears. Then she fell asleep.

She didn't wake up until it was dark. She was in her underwear, even though she didn't remember getting undressed. Her armpits smelled, and then she felt the soreness again. So she took a hot shower. Suddenly, she realized how hungry she was. So she got dressed and started to think about what to eat, when she got a text from Giselle: *Wondered how you were making out with all the snow.*

Giselle. So she called her and told her she had to come back to Ithaca because of the storm. "Are you hungry?" she asked.

"Not really. I just ate. But I'll go with you."

So they met at Nate's, a little pizza joint just off campus.

Vicky was glad to see Giselle, and was starting to feel better as she dug into her cold grinder.

"I thought you were a salad person?" Giselle said.

"Yeah, well every once in a while I need a little comfort food," she told her still chewing then taking another bite.

"Is everything okay? You look a little down."

You should have seen me a few hours ago, she thought. But she wasn't about to tell any of it even to Giselle. "It's nothing. I've just been trapped in an airport overnight and haven't eaten all day." Then she looked at her plate, ate a few chips, and looked back up. There was a sports story on the news, and it made her think of Nicholas, and her eyes got full and sad. Then she looked at Giselle, and Giselle saw.

"What's wrong? And don't tell me everything is okay."

She shook her head. "It's nothing. I was seeing this guy, and it didn't work out. That's all."

Giselle wasn't the sort to push. They both liked their privacy. The discussion would have ended right there. Vicky was about to change the subject anyway, mention a new book she saw on Persian Mystics on Fordham University Press, when the TV caught her eye again.

It was still the news, and a late-breaking story had just come in hot off the presses: *Multiple shooting in Utica. Four dead. Mob-related.* Then she saw the flash of a face off the blue and red sirens, right there on the TV in the middle of Nate's.

"Oh my god, that's him!"

"Who?" Giselle looked at her then saw that she was watching the TV behind her and turned around. Then she looked back at Vicky.

"Nicholas! The guy I was seeing!"

"Who? You mean one of the guys who got shot?! Are you freaking kidding me?!"

Vicky was tongue-tied for a moment, wondering if he was dead or alive or what had happened, and she had to find out.

"I gotta go," she said, getting up, still wearing her coat.

Giselle got up and put her coat on, throwing her scarf over her shoulder. "Wait up. Where?"

"To Utica."

Giselle chased after her. "Okay, but let me drive."

By the time they got there and found the scene, it was almost two hours later. There were still sirens, though, and at least a half dozen people. She saw the FBI jackets and the forensic experts dusting and carrying stuff out of the diner where the shootings had happened. She asked Giselle to wait in the car, while she got out and walked up to a man wearing one of those FBI jackets, writing in a pad.

"Excuse me, I know one of the men involved here tonight—at least I think I do—"

The man looked up for a split second and pointed his thumb over his shoulder, "Talk to him." Then he went back to writing.

So Vicky went over to the other man, who was talking to what looked like one of the forensics people.

When they were done, she caught his eye. "I'm a friend of one of the people involved here tonight," she repeated.

Suddenly, she had his full attention. He looked at her with that serious cop look that she'd seen so many times in her father. "What's you name, miss?"

"Victoria Scardo."

"And who was your friend?"

Was. It hit her right between the eyes. "Nicholas Barczynski."

He raised his eyebrows. "How do you know Special Agent Barczynski?"

Special Agent?! So he was one of the good guys? It made her feel warm and terrible all at the same time. "We're friends. We met at the airport, struck up a conversation. I live in Ithaca. I'm a professor at Cornell. I saw what happened on TV, and I drove up to see if he was okay." Then she gritted her teeth and asked. "So is he okay?"

"Yeah, he's fine. I don't know how. He must have a guardian angel."

She heaved out a sigh of relief and smiled like she'd just won the lottery. She looked at the man's name tag. "Thank you Agent Colón."

"No problem."

"Where is he?"

"Headed back home to Miami. He was pretty anxious to see his wife. He was kind of shaken up."

His wife. "Thank you again," she said, happy he was alive and that he was one of the good guys. A cop like her dad. Sort of. And she began to realize what she had lost and felt as sad as she ever had.

She was quiet on the car ride back, telling Giselle that he was okay and that she was relieved but not much more. When she got home, she sent him a text: *I saw what happened and drove to Utica, spoke to Agent Colón. Boy did I get things wrong! I'm so proud of you. Much love, Vicky.*

She waited for him to answer, but he didn't. So she took a shower and went to bed. It was all replaying in her head, and she knew it would be for a long time.

It was a cold night, and she slept deeply. When she tumbled out of bed in the morning, it felt like it had all been a dream. She used the bathroom and went downstairs, not even bothering to change out of her pajamas. *I'll get over this,* she thought. *It didn't work out, but it wasn't a mistake.* Then she got herself a cup of coffee and looked out through the cut-glass window of her large front door. Sitting there, she could see Nicholas's face. A dream. But then—wait—no—it really was Nicholas's face! He was there, at her front door!

She practically spit out her coffee, swallowing hard before she got up from her counter stool and went over to let him in. Moving as quickly as she could, she spilled coffee on her leg on the way. Suddenly, she couldn't remember which way to turn the lock, until finally, she got it open.

There was a blast of cold air, and he stepped in and shook his coat, even though there was no snow on it.

"Oh my god, what are doing here?!" she said, smiling at him with an uncertain wonder verging on joy.

"I was in the neighborhood."

Those dumb lines of his. It was one of the things she knew she'd miss. Then she reached out and hugged him, trying not to spill more coffee. "I'm so glad you're okay."

He seemed taken aback for a second—he was reserved like that—then he hugged her back tightly.

They went over to the center island of her kitchen, the one nod to modernity in the old house, and sat down at the bar stools and talked, him in a sharp suit with his English leather shoes, and her in her pajamas, just rolled out of bed, not even through her first cup of coffee.

And now, he told her everything.

"I was a cop for fifteen years. I started at the Newark Police Department then moved over to the NYPD, got my gold shield. By the time I retired, I was burned out. I was already flipping houses on the side—Jersey City, Newark, Union City—so I started a second career. Then I met Pam. We got married, ended up moving to Miami. She started an antiques store. Then one day, the FBI contacted me. They needed an inside man for a sting operation between the mob up in Utica and the boys down in Miami. I'd be perfect for it. They needed someone with police creds who knew about house restoration. They already knew me through some mutual friends in the Newark office. My marriage was already in pieces, so I said okay. Only it turned into something much bigger.

"I helped them figure that out—that they weren't just skimming off the contract work but were smuggling drugs in from South America with the building materials. Only they didn't bother to let me in on the secret until after the fact. I'm still a little pissed at Colón about that, but they figured the fewer the people who knew, the better.

"I didn't like lying to you. But I had no choice. I couldn't say anything. For your own safety. And mine. Most of what I told you was actually true anyway."

She nodded.

"So they appointed me a Special Agent. I brought the cash up every week, did the fake inspections, filed the fake reports, laid the groundwork. Turns out Jo Jo, one the goons up in Utica who was supposed to count the money, actually was skimming. They found out and killed him, but not before he tried to blame me. So they figured I was probably in on it and decided to kill me too. Colón—you met Colón—wanted to get more evidence before we dropped the hammer, but there was no time."

She nodded again.

"It was a bit of a surprise, but it all ended up going down last night." Then he smiled a little. "I actually took down Jimmy Bevelaqua, the local capo. I shot him in the knee, that lousy prick. I'm probably going to get a citation for bravery. It's funny, when I was a cop, I never fired my gun even once. And last night, I killed two men." He looked at her, his soul bare, and she knew it. "I came pretty close to getting killed myself," he added, almost as an afterthought.

"Lying there on the floor, a couple of guys dead, my own life on the line, I realized—I realized I didn't love my wife. You're the one I love. You're the one I want to be with."

Then he pulled out a piece of paper and handed it to her. "I filed those divorce papers with the county clerk in Miami this morning. That's why I had to fly down." He paused for a second. "I also wanted to tell Pam in person. I owed her that."

Vicky held the paper and stared at him. She felt lightheaded and dizzy. She loved him, she knew that. But it was all so up-in-the-air. He lived in Miami; she split her time between Ithaca and Washington. Was he proposing? Did he want to live with her? What were his plans? She didn't even know if she was going to get tenure or inherit the dictionary project.

Then he took her face in his hands and kissed her, and none of it mattered.

"They offered me a job in Washington," he told her. "I think I can arrange it so that I only need to be there three days a week. Colón owes me. The rest of the time, I can run my contracting business on the side." He looked around. "I think I'll start with this house." Then her eyes followed his as he looked over at the fireplace, where she would sit curled up alone reading books on cold winter nights.

There would be someone else there now with her, and she wouldn't be alone anymore. And neither would he. Wherever they were.

To see our other great titles,
visit us at:

BLACKBIRD BOOKS
www.bbirdbooks.com